BAD BEARS GO VISITING

An **IRVING** & **MUKTUK** Story

by **Daniel Pinkwater**

illustrations by **Jill Pinkwater**

Houghton Mifflin Company
Boston 2007

To Edward Weiss,
webmaster, genius,
and friend.

www.houghtonmifflinbooks.com

The text of this book is set in
13-point Leawood.
The illustrations were created with felt-tip
marker and ink on Bristol board.

Library of Congress
Cataloging-in-Publication Data
Pinkwater, Daniel Manus, 1941–
Bad bears go visiting / by Daniel Pinkwater;
illustrations by Jill Pinkwater.
p. cm.
Summary: Irving and Muktuk, two polar
bears, enjoy themselves so much when Larry
comes to visit them that the next time they
escape from the zoo in Bayonne, New Jersey,
they decide to pay a visit themselves.
ISBN-13: 978-0-618-43126-7 (hardcover)
ISBN-10: 0-618-43126-8 (hardcover)
[1. Polar bears—Fiction. 2. Bears—Fiction.
3. Social skills—Fiction.
4. Zoos—Fiction. 5. Humorous stories.]
I. Pinkwater, Jill, ill. II. Title.
PZ7.P6335Vis 2007
[E]—dc22
2006009819

Manufactured in China
SCP 10 9 8 7 6 5 4 3 2 1

It is a beautiful summer evening. The zoo
has closed for the day. The animals have
been fed. Irving and Muktuk are cheating
each other at cards.

There is a knock at the door.

"Who can that be?" Irving asks Muktuk.

"It is Larry! Our friend!" Muktuk says. "Larry, what are you doing here?"

"I have come to visit you," Larry says.

"Visit us?"

"Yes. A visit is when you go to some-one's house and have a nice time. And I have brought you a present," Larry says.

"A present?"

"It is a cake. It has little fishes on it," Larry says.

"Are the fishes made of sugar icing?"
Muktuk asks.
  "No. They are real fish," Larry says.
  "Yummo!"

The bears eat the cake with the little fishes on it.

"What do we do now?" Irving and Muktuk ask.

"We have fun," Larry says. "We have fun, and then I go home. Would you like to play volleyball?"

The bears play volleyball, two against one. Naturally, Irving and Muktuk cheat.

"Now we sit around and chat pleasantly," Larry says.
The bears sit around and chat pleasantly.
"The penguins in this zoo are afraid of us," Irving says.
"They sure are," Muktuk says.

"I hope you don't do things to frighten
them," Larry says.

"Oh, no, never," Irving and Muktuk say.

"I had a good time," Larry says. "I will go home now."

"Thank you for visiting us," Irving and Muktuk say.

"Visits are nice."

It is the next evening. The zoo has closed. The animals have been fed.

"Do you want to play cards?" Irving asks Muktuk. "Do you want to frighten the penguins? Shall we escape from the zoo?"

"It is a nice evening," Muktuk says. "Let's escape."

"That will call for sneaking," Irving says.

Irving and Muktuk sneak out of their room. They sneak out of the polar bear enclosure. They sneak through the zoo. They sneak through the gate.

Though polar bears are very large, they are among the best sneakers in the animal kingdom.

Once outside, Irving and Muktuk run down the street. They turn many corners and run down many more streets. Soon they have left the zoo far behind.

"That was excellent sneaking and running," Muktuk says.
"What shall we do now?"
"You want to look for some blueberry muffins?" Irving asks.
"We always do that," Muktuk says.

"Sneak into a fish market?"
"Then they will holler at us when we go back to the zoo," Muktuk says.
"We could go visiting," Irving says.

"Yes! Visiting is nice," Muktuk says.

"Who shall we visit?" Irving asks.

Muktuk looks up and down the street. "There are lots of houses. Let's pick one."

"This is a nice house. Let's visit here."

"Yes. This looks like a nice house for a visit," Muktuk says.
"Knock on the door."

"Wait!" Irving says. "We should have a present."

"Oh, yes, a present!" Muktuk says.

"We don't have a present," Irving says. "Let's look around for one."

Steve and Loretta Beachball and their little daughter, Sylvia, are enjoying an evening at home. They have cleared away the supper dishes and are watching the weightlifting championship on television. They are all wearing their house slippers and eating popcorn.

There is a loud knock on the door. Little Sylvia looks out the window.
"There are polar bears at the door," Sylvia says.
"See what they want," Mr. Beachball says.

"Hello," Irving and Muktuk say.
"We have come to visit you."
"They have come to visit us,"
Sylvia calls to her parents.

"We have brought a present," Irving says.
"It is a bush," Muktuk says.
"It has little flowers on it," Irving says.

"Thank you," Mrs. Beachball says. "It is just like the bushes we have in our front yard."

"We should have a snack," Irving says.

"Do you have a cake with little fishes on top?" Muktuk asks.

"We have some doughnuts," Mr. Beachball says. "We could put sardines on them."

"Yummo!"

"Little Sylvia," Mr. Beachball says. "Would you go out to the kitchen and prepare doughnuts with sardines for our guests?"

"While you do that, we will sit around and chat pleasantly," Irving says.

"While you are in the kitchen, you might want to make a telephone call," Mrs. Beachball says.

"I understand," little Sylvia Beachball says.

"In a little while, we will play volleyball," Muktuk says.

Little Sylvia Beachball returns from the kitchen with doughnuts and sardines.

"Yummo!" Irving and Muktuk say.

"Everything is taken care of," Little Sylvia tells her parents.

The Beachballs' living room is small for a volleyball game with polar bears. There is a certain amount of damage.

"We are winning, even though it is three against two," Irving whispers to Muktuk.

"And without even cheating," Muktuk whispers to Irving.

Then there are flashing lights, and sirens, and someone speaking through an electric bullhorn.

"It is Captain Hare, of the police," the voice says. "Come out with your paws up."

"The police are here," Irving says.

"Do they want us to come out with our paws up?" Muktuk asks.

"Yes," Irving says.

"As usual," Muktuk says.

"We had a good time," Irving and Muktuk tell the Beachballs.
"Please come and visit us next time."

Outside, the police are waiting, and Mr. Goldberg, the bear keeper, and the head zookeeper, and the zoo bus.

"I think that went very well," Irving tells Muktuk.
"It is nice to have a visit, and it is nice to make a visit," Muktuk tells Irving.